I0726562

CODY GOODFELLOW

EXILED FROM MIDDLE EARTH: HOW FANTASY FAILED US

I remember tears welling up in my eyes at the beginning of Peter Jackson's *The Fellowship Of The Ring*, when Frodo confronts Gandalf, upon his belated return to the Shire. When Gandalf replies that "a wizard always arrives precisely when he means to," all the love and wonder Tolkien's books had given me came flooding back. For so many of us, *The Lord Of The Rings* was the cornerstone upon which all modern fantasy rests, and to see it brought so lovingly to life was a visceral, overwhelming experience which only escalated with the successive entries in the trilogy. For me, it was much more, for it forced me to confront unexamined feelings for my father, who died when I was eight.

I remember my father always had the Tolkien calendar on his kitchen wall, the lavish Hildebrandt brothers artwork burning scenes into my mind long before I understood their context. He had two cats, Gandalf and Gollum. I remember seeing Bakshi's Lord Of The Rings in the theater with him and watching The Time Machine on TV, and getting Conan comics and visiting a park to see concrete dinosaur statues, the last time I saw him.

Only later did I understand how vital a refuge fantasy was for my father, in a dreary world that never seemed to give him a break. Always relegated to the dimmest corner of the local library or B. Dalton Bookseller, a creaky spinner rack in the drugstore, the graveyard shift on local TV, any glimpse of fantasy was like a transmission from another world more magical and pure than our own, and balm for souls rubbed raw by the button-down bullshit of modern life.

Fast-forward forty years, and, of course, fantasy fandom has become a monolithic mainstream phenomenon. We all hunger for escape, and epic fantasy is a staple. Even people who can't name their own elected representatives and don't know when World War 2 happened, know all about the Siege of Gondor and the Red Wedding. It is a golden age of escapism, and yet fantasy remains a stagnant cesspool of cliché, bloated excess, and reactionary, toxic fandom. The thing intended to deliver us from the pressure cooker of modern life has become as fraught with frustration, entitlement, and bigotry as the world we sought to escape from.

As I'm hardly the first to observe, much of the problem lies in fantasy itself. Born out of the romantic, decadent and exoticism movements of the late nineteenth century, fantasy fiction as a genre had its roots as much in the Arabian Nights as in the European culture heroes, from the Scandinavian sagas and Arthurian myths. The rejection of modernity and rediscovery of primal attributes in seminal fantasy by Saki, T.H. White, Lord Dunsany and others, the yearning for strange perfumes and foreign shores, for quests and tests of valor and bouts of courtly romance was a luxury spared for those who had successfully foisted their will upon the rest of the world, and languished in the comfortable leisure hours bought by colonialism and white supremacy. If they expected to be swept away from the mundane, they also expected to have their cherished inner myths valorized. From the childlike Aryan race theory of Robert E. Howard to the elaborate Christian allegory of C.S. Lewis, early fantasy took readers to far-off places while validating the core values they brought with them from home. Witness the furious backlash against the casting of Jason Momoa as the last cinematic incarnation of Conan, and you see how zealously the white core readership cherishes its fantasy icons not as vehicles for experiencing the Other, but as reflections of their own perpetually imperiled whiteness.

If Tolkien stirred our noblest aspirations, he also created a benign propaganda that mythologized cultural differences until nationalities became species, and denied basic humanity to its antagonists, rendering the defense of the divine right of kings into a Manichean conflict between absolute light and absolute darkness—arguably, in spite of his denials, an allegory for Europe's agonizing crusade against Hitler.

As noted contrarian David Brin observed in an essay coinciding with Jackson's grandiose adaptation of *Lord Of The Rings*, the humans and their allies worship at the altar of absolute hereditary rule, and libel the one agent of merit, inclusion and technological progress in Middle Earth. Certainly, the notion that the land might incarnate itself in the form of a devoted ruler is a beautiful conceit, but it's only the most richly embroidered defense of a myth that's brought little but tribulation and tragedy, in the real world. If one were to ask the Saudi Crown Prince in a candid moment about the butchery of Jamal Khashoggi only this month, he would no doubt clothe his rationalization by noting that the *Washington Post* journalist dismembered with bone saws in the Saudi consulate in Turkey was just another orc threatening his divinely ordained kingdom.

While lauded by critics and showered with awards, Jackson's film adaptations were assailed by Tolkien-cult ingrates pining for Tom Bombadil, then pilloried for shoehorning in female characters with actual agency and blowing out gateway fantasy drug *The Hobbit* into a plodding trilogy of videogame cut-scenes and high-res irrelevance.

Aside from gleaming outliers like Ursula K. LeGuin's Earthsea trilogy and Gene Wolfe's Book Of The New Sun, epic fantasy since Tolkien seems to have taken up all his worst excesses without capturing his ineffable grandeur. Virtually all earlier incarnations of the genre were forgotten, despite the Ballantine Adult Fantasy line's valiant attempt to capitalize on the boom by reviving Smith, Dunsany, Hodgson, Eddison, Beckford and others, in favor of the monolithic saga that foisted a humble peasant into the role of upstart challenger against some obligatory dark eminence from the east. Reactions to Tolkien tended to boil away the engrossing complexity into a stew of YA destiny-porn like Lloyd Alexander's *Prydain Chronicles* or David Ebbings' *Belgariad*, or drag an all-too-human element into the plot in troublesome, if not always edifying ways. Stephen Donaldson's Thomas Covenant books, in particular, brought an ugly streak of self-loathing misogyny into his fantasy realm, in the form of a protagonist who utterly rejects the lofty role chosen for him by the guardians of The Land, only to accept it by committing a rape

so monstrous, it obliterates any meta-message about fantasy vs. reality it might've hoped to send. Marion Zimmer Bradley's *Mists Of Avalon*, long championed as a feminist take on the Arthurian cycle, has since been condemned in light of its author's creepy sexual proclivities, and John Norman's risible *Gor* series endures primarily as a primer for sexual dominance play.

White men still rule modern fantasy, and women and people of color are still denigrated as magical elfin dream-girls and subhuman beast-creatures, respectively. In order to repay its influences while jockeying for mainstream success, the quest itself becomes a bloated mcguffin, as in the preposterously long grift of Robert Jordan's *Wheel Of Time* series, and the idealized depictions of good and evil have become no more illuminating, but far less inspiring, with injections of banal and base human nature. Martin's *Song Of Ice And Fire* is a morbidly obese but still-incomplete drag that only television can bring to a conclusion, its plot a brutalist soap opera following equally unworthy rulers as they wreak havoc and desolation not to exterminate some stereotypical evil, but for power itself. While Tolkien resisted the reduction of his magnum opus to a fairy tale about World War 2, Martin has embraced fan theories that his epic of incest and internecine warfare symbolizes contemporary political dithering in the face of global climate change, seeking to shake us to a realization we've bitterly resisted absorbing from the daily news. In too many ways, the real world has invaded our dreams. If Sauron and the orcs were to invade Westeros, they would be welcomed as liberators.

But nowhere is the regressive nature of modern fantasy more blatant than J.K. Rowling's Harry Potter series. Justly lauded for inspiring millions of young readers to embark upon more ambitious reading journeys, yet as high fantasy, it reflects a turning away from the crucible of conflict into the warm cloister of an uncannily nurturing boarding school that tacks every hoary fantasy cliché onto the real thrill of being every teacher's pet in an adverb-larded parade of inevitable accolades and cake-walk quests. That Harry Potter's cozy, saccharine

comfort food commands such unswerving loyalty among ostensible adults suggests that too many readers dream less of a harrowing quest that will test their mettle, and more of simply staying in school and having all the answers to the tests given to them because they're destined to win, anyway.

The biggest problem is the way we've been trained to escape, and what we're escaping from. The medium has too long been subject to the publisher-pushed notion that fantasy must come in multi-volume door-stop epics to be taken seriously. We're not seeking adventure to leaven a dull existence, so much as seeking to escape real chaos and conflict bordering on the fantastical. When America becomes Mordor and Sauron a New York reality show slumlord, fantasy realms become our new homeland.

The sheer volume of fantasy offerings in every medium makes escapism not a diversion from life, but a career, albeit an unpaid one, and less and less of a rewarding one.

The embarrassment of riches and fool's gold has left us overstimulated and spoiled, incapable of simply losing oneself as in childhood, even as the pressure we all feel in life drives us to bring the grievances of workaday life into our books, movies and video games and social media conversations about them.

The deep personal sense of nostalgia attached to our favorite works, long taken for granted and ruthlessly exploited by corporate media, dictates that fantasy should take us to other worlds while always looking, walking and talking like us, and so we've sealed ourselves in a bubble, huffing our favorite dreams like so many canned farts. Small wonder then, that so many who've never identified as racist or sexist find themselves raging at their peers as cherished fantasy properties are retconned, rebooted or otherwise adulterated from the "pure" forms they grew up with; if everything in life is stagnating or being taken away, it might feel like they're really raping your childhood, but get a fucking grip.

The only reason all too many corporate purveyors of fantasy are in the business is because you're buying what they're selling. If you walk past the $28.00 tomes and sprawling movie franchises to seek out artists who create passionately on the fringes of the market, you'll find that pure love, that escape from this world, that you've been craving.

We say that to survive its own commercial success, fantasy must welcome everyone and embrace and let us empathize with the Other, and not reinforce dangerous jingoistic fantasies. We say that true escapism should playfully speak to our real world anxieties in the sublimated symbolism of dreams, resisting bald political parable and instead taking us to new arenas to challenge the enemies that go faceless and unnamed in our wretched waking lives. We say that the best fantasies are not epic, self-serious slabs of verbal masonry, but the sort of short, sharp daydreams that shock us awake, and let us see with new eyes.

We are tired of Tolkien and mad at Martin, but dreaming of Smith and Dunsany, longing for Leiber, and mad for Moorcock. In all of these, we see pure imagination win out over warmed-over Euro-centric myth cycles, where we are all equally foreign invaders. In Leiber, we see a love of swashbuckling fantasy for its own sake, nevertheless imbued with poignant critiques of humanity worthy of the most lauded mainstream literature. In Moorcock, we witness the deconstruction of the archetypal fantasy hero and divorce his obligatory quest from flimsy and dangerous labels of good and evil, unmasked as merely Law and Chaos. In all of these, we see the short story and novelette elevated to mythic status, and all the bullshit burned away. With this issue, we hope to rediscover what we've always loved about conventional fantasy tropes while destroying the tired conventions themselves and reigniting in our readers a love of strange shores and alien dreams. And as always with this labor of love, we hope to do our fathers, and our mothers, proud.

UNCLE KRUST'S DUNGEON BASTARD'S GUIDE TO FANTASTIC BEASTS

CODY GOODFELLOW

GHºULS

—WHAT CANNIBALISM ACTUALLY TURNS YOU INTO.
—EMO-NIHILIST OPEN-MIC HOGS.
—HYSTERICAL ABOUT PC ABUSE OF RESURRECTION SPELLS.
—IF YOU ENCOUNTER THEM AT ALL, YOU'RE DUNGEON-CRAWLING TOO SLOWLY.

ELF

—ENDLESS LECTURES ABOUT HOW ALL THEIR GEAR IS BETTER BECAUSE IT'S "ENCHANTED."
—WHAT YOU THINK THE FRENCH ARE LIKE, IF YOU'VE NEVER BEEN TO FRANCE.
—"ENCHANTS" ITEMS BY FARTING ON THEM.
—EXHAUSTING.

GºBLINS

—HOARD CONSISTS ENTIRELY OF ELVISH REVENGE PORN.
—BASICALLY JUST PERVY ORCS.
—LOOK NOTHING LIKE THEIR TINDER PROFILES.
—WORTH LETTING DEFEAT YOU, FOR THE AWESOME SONG THEY'LL SING ABOUT COOKING YOU.

OGRE

—WHAT YOU THINK CANNIBALISM TURNS YOU INTO.
—ON A VEGAN DIET; ONLY EATS VEGANS.
—SUCKERS FOR "GOT YOUR NOSE" GAG (TRY IT!).
—WILL GRIND YOUR BONES TO MAKE HIS BREAD, BUT THEN GET A PIZZA
  WHILE YOUR BREAD MOLDS.

TRºLL

—CONSTANTLY CARPING ABOUT INCIVILITY OF PEOPLE HE EATS.
—ATTACKS FEMALES IN PARTY FIRST, FOR DRESSING SLUTTY.
—USES OWN FECES AS WEAPON, FURNITURE, SUBSTANTIVE DEBATE.
—HYSTERICAL ABOUT PLAYER CHARACTER DOMINANCE OF POPULAR
  CULTURE.

DRºW

—WHAT YOU THINK SCANDINAVIANS ARE LIKE... AND YOU'RE RIGHT.
—GOTH AF.
—ARMOR CLASS 0 ENCHANTED PLATE; ARMOR CLASS 9 FEELINGS.
—MAY SPARE YOUR LIFE IF YOU SAY THE RIGHT THINGS ABOUT THE
  SUSPIRIA REMAKE.

BRºWNIE

—OFTEN FOUND SELLING COOKIES OUTSIDE HALFLING DISPENSARIES.
—WILL MAKE SHOES FOR COPPER PIECES... TINY, TINY SHOES.
—CHAOTIC NEUTRAL IN THE STREETS; CHAOTIC EVIL IN THE SHEETS.
—HOARD CONSISTS ENTIRELY OF MY LITTLE PONY FIGURINES.

TEARS OF THE ELOHIM

JOHN R FULTZ

WHEN THE ELOHIM CAME TO THE VALLEY OF SACRED BONES, THEY FOUND THE BODIES OF GIANTS LYING IN SCATTERED HEAPS.

HERE, AMONG THE BROKEN AND PLUNDERED TOMBS OF THEIR ANCESTORS, THE LAST OF THE MOUNTAIN GOD'S CHILDREN HAD MADE THEIR FINAL STAND. AND LOST.

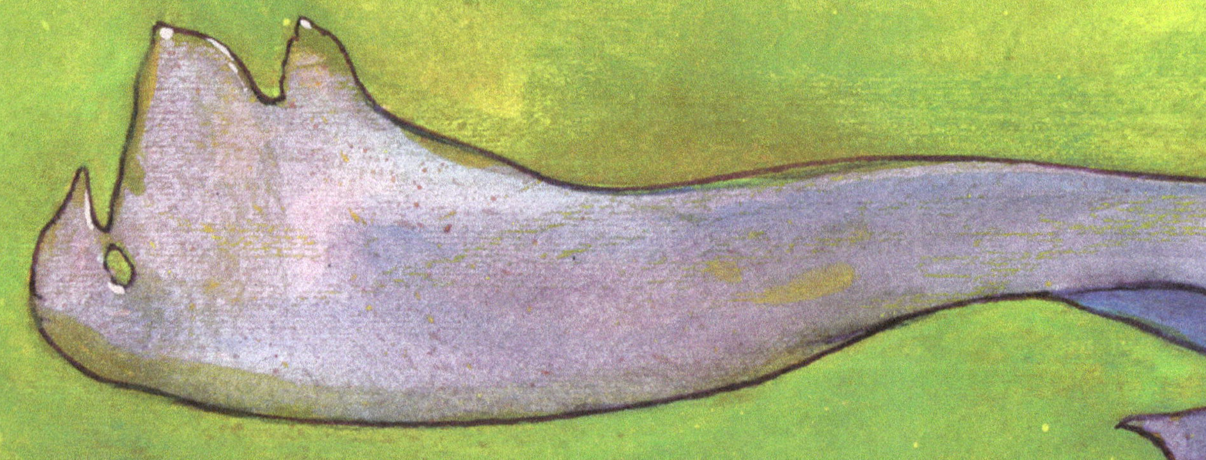

Twilight spilled like giants' blood across the sky. A score of slaughtered behemoths lay rotting among the violated bones of their grandfathers. Blinking silver eyes against a carrion wind, the Elohim wept as they walked among the giant corpses. Swarms of flies and vultures fled from the gleam of their bright armor and shields.

The mouth of the valley sparkled with the campfires of men, three conjoined armies of southern savages who had won the nine-day battle. The Elohim had watched them fight from on high, never dreaming that such frail and short-lived beings could destroy the last of the Mountain God's people. With foolish valor and reckless determination, the men had brought down each giant like a swarm of biting insects might bring down a lion. They died in great numbers, yet gloried in their own mortality, laughing at death, driving their spears into gigantic hearts, their bronze blades piercing brains larger than their whole bodies. So the men fought and so the giants died.

The Elohim had watched it all with dry eyes from their place about the Mountain God's throne. Now they walked among the bloody dead and their tears flowed freely.

The triumphant forces had blended into a single army and burned their dead in great conflagrations. Tonight they drank dry the barrels of ale that camp followers brought to the battlefield. They gathered in their thousands about the great tent of their king. The strong drink made them forget the pain of their wounds as they sang ancient songs of valor to honor their dead. The great victory had not been without cost. Yet the strongest and fittest warriors had survived to pledge their lives to him they now called the High King.

The great camp roared with celebration. A consort of cooks served bowls of lamb stew boiled in a giant's skull large as a cauldron. Men gladly accepted the invitations of the working maidens, who slipped among the tents adding coins to their purses one by one. In the great madness of their victory, none of them heard

EXILED FROM MIDDLE EARTH

the distant watchman's horn as he announced the coming of the Elohim.

"Tomorrow," the High King told his circle of captains, "we will plunder the deepest of the ancient tombs." The captains cheered their lord, raised their goblets, and swilled the ale that dulled their senses. "The gold and jewels buried here in ancient times will allow us to found an eternal empire of men. A High Kingdom to stand above all others." The men would have cheered again for their lord, if not for the gleaming of strange colors that outshone the pavilion's torchlight and drew their attention.

The glimmering Elohim entered the mouth of the tent, a dozen figures lithe and tall. They stood head and shoulders above men, but they were not giants. They were graceful and beautiful where the giants had been misshapen and ugly. Their ears tapered to delicate points beneath ornate helms. Their eyes glistened like stars underwater, perhaps because of their lambent tears.

The Elohim stood wordless and gleaming before the lord of men, silent as moonbeams. All eyes had turned to the bright ones, and the High King raised his foaming cup.

"Elves?" he cried out. In his drunkenness, he laughed at them. "Have the Gates of Faerie opened in this cursed valley tonight?"

The foremost of the Elohim spoke. His voice was like a soft wind, yet the king heard him perfectly. "We come from the court of the Mountain God."

The High King smiled and rubbed his black beard. He sank back into the fur-lined divan that served as a traveling throne and spread his great arms.

"I know not this god of which you speak, but you are most welcome here. Come and share in our victory feast!"

"Allow us to praise your valiant nature," said the Elohim. "You have won a great victory this day. Men have bested giants once and for all."

The Elohim walked deeper into the pavilion, and each of their footprints left a stain of giant's blood across the king's pale carpets.

"You speak of praise, yet your eyes swim with tears," said the king. "Do you weep for the giants who died here—or the men?"

"Neither," said the foremost Elohim.

The High King reached for the handle of his great broadsword. Its blade was stained dark with the ichor of giants.

"Why then do you weep?" he snarled.

"We weep for ourselves," said the Elohim. "For what we must do. Your victory was fairly won, but the tombs of the giant-kings must not be disturbed. It is the god's will."

The eyes of the drunken captains squinted as the Elohim drew their silver swords.

"Those tombs belong to us now," said the High King. He lifted his heavy blade to point at the Elohim. "Many men died in this valley, but we are still thousands strong. You are but a dozen. You cannot slay us all."

The foremost Elohim lowered his perfect face. Fallen tears glistened like droplets of gold across his breastplate. "Yet that is what we must do," he said. "We must kill every last one of you, as you killed every last giant. Therefore we weep."

The Elohim danced about the High King and their swords flashed like sparks. Before any man could move to aid him, they carved him into a hundred pieces. His valiant blood rained across the feasting table and the faces of the horrified captains.

At last the men broke from their spell and scrambled for spear, axe, and sword. They rushed upon the dancing Elohim one at a time, then in groups, yet always they died beneath the rain of silver blades. The Elohim kept dancing, and a red storm filled the valley.

They danced a whirlwind of death, blades spinning, eyes flashing.

Weeping, they danced.

EXILED FROM MIDDLE EARTH

DRAGONFIRE

CHAD STROUP

UPON SEIZING HIS BELOVED PRINCESS GENEVIEVE, ERØJER THE ROSEDRAGON LOOKED FORWARD TO FINALLY SHEDDING HIS VIRGINITY. LITTLE DID HE KNOW, LOVE SELDOM GOES AS PLANNED.

Summoning all the courage he possessed, he left the comfort of his cave and soared to Castle G'leta, just beyond the Isle of Viista, where he spotted the princess picking wyldflowers in the field just beyond the castle gates, then swooped in and snatched her up before the king's peons knew what to do with themselves.

All save for the dreaded knight, Sir Chad. The hero of the castle charged out on his steed, sword clenched firmly in mailed fist, his thick, dark mane like a cape fluttering behind him. The horse's speed was no match for the power of Erøjer's wings and the wind, but still, Sir Chad pursued.

Erøjer envied the knight's prowess, not just in battle, but also in bed, so the rumors had spread throughout the kingdom. No woman could resist him. Nor, so the whispers told, could any man.

Sir Chad's gallant predecessors had slain all remaining Diamondwings, leaving the Rosedragons to reach the age of fertility with no way to seek muliebral warmth. When Sir Chad finally arrived to rescue Princess Genevieve, Erøjer would leave him a roasted swine, a grisly banquet offering for his rotten king. The time of rejection and defeat had come to an end.

Rosedragons couldn't help being introverts. Hibernation did that to a fellow. Still, throughout the years, Erøjer had aligned himself with a few other Rosedragons. The Wizards of Mount Fir'Shann, they dubbed themselves. Erøjer had never met the others in the scaly flesh, but they hissed to one another via the echoes that bounced off the damp cavern walls. Their daily chinwags soothed Erøjer's feelings of isolation. He knew there were others ready to take up his cause, when the time came.

And that time would be soon.

But for now, he'd remain down below. His cave brought him comfort, his mountain of gold the kingdom's most expensive bed. Erøjer had worked so hard to build his pile of riches—scorching towns and their folk until not even embers remained—but his treasures and the methods by which they'd been acquired failed to impress Genevieve. What could he possibly do to get her—or any princess—to acknowledge him? Rosedragons didn't know poetry from pottery, and—despite the name of their breed—they found flowers quite disagreeable. He'd trade away every last coin, if just one of these ungrateful wenches would give themselves to him willingly. And for eternity.

Erøjer decided a nap was in order. Slumber was sure to bring clarity.

As the Rosedragon traveled to the Land of Nod, he dreamt of Sir Chad. Yet something had changed about his foe. The knight's lovely long locks were now fair and curled, flowing as if the wind carried them. He wore not a suit of armor, but a bodiced petticoat, laced tight with golden thread. He called himself Lady Charlotte. *Charlotte the Harlot.* He yearned not to slay but to *be* slayed.

Erøjer awoke, every scale on his serpentine body quivering. He vowed to abandon all pretense of seduction. Starting today, Rosedragons didn't ask politely. They took whatever they wanted.

Princess Genevieve was chained to a jagged, crooked stone with chains and leather thongs, gagged with a glob of dragonspit, a thick, grey gel that filled her entire mouth. Tears fell from her eyes, suicide jumpers from a lonely bridge.

"Princess Genevieve, my object of desire, why do you not adore me?" Erøjer fancied his voice an intimidating boom, but the flowery words were marred by the pathetic squeak from his wicked underbite. All remaining confidence went straight down the shit pit.

The princess squealed and squirmed. Her bosom rose and fell. Erøjer stood on his hind legs, showed off the impressive physique he'd worked so hard to build, revealed his pleasure wyrm below.

He unsheathed one ferocious claw, dug it tenderly into the princess's mouth to remove the dragonspit. It plopped to the ground like fresh placenta. Genevieve vomited and gasped for air. Her eyes went straight to his pleasure wyrm, and every ounce of fear she'd been harboring transformed into maddening mirth. Her laughs were icicles scraping against the deepest crevices of Erøjer's eardrums.

"You find something amusing, woman?"

"I've never seen a dragon's pizzle." Genevieve tried to lift her bound hand to point at his pleasure wyrm. "It's like a man's, only smaller."

Erøjer paused, unsure how to react to such a ruinous insult. He did the one thing that came naturally. With one swipe of his claw, he tore the princess from the stone, snapping leather, chains, flesh, and bone as if they were made of paper. All but one chain, which still clung to the princess's detached left arm.

Erøjer lifted her toward his face. A geyser of blood spilled to the ground, staining his precious coins. The princess's echoing screams filled the cave, and Erøjer wondered if the other Wizards of Mount Fir'Shann could hear. He hoped, prayed they'd be jealous.

Before Genevieve could beg for what remained of her life, Erøjer opened his gaping maw and tossed her in.

A crunch, a gulp, and a belch.

He'd barely had time to begin digesting her, before he heard the neigh of a horse off in the distance, then the battle cry of a warrior.

Sir Chad.

Something stirred deep within Erøjer. The truth. He steadied himself. The Rosedragon had many centuries to look forward to, many more riches to hoard, and he wished for someone with whom he could share his warmth.

Sir Chad would surely understand in time.

Erøjer did not plan to die a virgin.

WIGHT KNIGHT
NATHAN CANSON

SOLONJA RACED BACK TO CAMP, THE STO-
LEN SWORD STILL FINDING BALANCE IN
HER GRIP. SHE WAS CERTAIN HER PURSU-
ERS LOST THE TRAIL WHEN SHE FORDED
THE ONYX RIVER THAT SOME SAID CURSED
ALL WHO SWAM IT. JUNGLE BRUSH BLED
OUT INTO THE STONY FOOTHILLS WHERE
HER SAFETY WOULD BE ASSURED. BUT
TONES OF BESTIAL DISTRESS STOPPED HER
SHORT; SHE CREPT AROUND THE CAMP TO
SURVEY WHAT NIGHTMARE INTRUDED.

A brutish, muscled male form stood beside the cold, ashen campfire remains. He gripped a winged wyrm twice his size by the throat. Its tongue lolled from its mouth. Bloodstained saliva oozed from its slackened jaws. Solonja could see debris from the drugged meal scattered at their feet. Her muscles tensed in silent fury, poised to spring.

"Banish your fear," the brawny figure said, as it turned toward the foliage beneath the mountain coconut palms where Solonja hid. Though his body was muscle and sinew, clad only in boots, fur gauntlets and skirt, his face...its face...held the sickly green-black hue of animated death. Solonja felt her heart constrict at the sight of its inhuman visage.

Nevertheless, she persisted. Solojna stepped forth into the clearing to face the ruined warrior. By now, the stolen sword had acclimated to her hand. She raised it into the air and uttered, "Let her go."

"Poor lass," he responded. "You who have been raised in this society. A slave to their kind. You know of no other life. I will show you. I will set you free."

Solonja couldn't imagine what its ravings meant, and she said so. "I am a free woman, charged to serve the Goddess of Flame."

He burst into hideous laughter. "Before my doom, I was a paladin. My service to a higher power was a shackle born from lies. Just as yours."

So, this thing had been a knight. How hard it must have fallen to exist in such a half-life state, creeping into campsites and drugging dragonspawn?

"In your world," he said, "dragons hold all property, social privilege, and authority. You are bred to ride them. Help them fight their wars. Obey their cruel whims."

Solonja's mind reeled. What was he carrying on about? She began to strafe to the knight's left bit by bit, to give his sword arm less chance at a clean arc.

"Long ago," he continued, "men and dragons were equal."

The wyrm in the knight's arms spasmed. Whether it was regaining strength or preparing to die, none will ever know. For when it lurched, the knight swung his fell sword in a swift cut. Solonja gasped at the sight of the beast's body falling limp, while the head and a length of its neck hung from its killer's grip. Blood dripped from the blade, soiling the earth.

"Another blow to the Dracriarchy!" cried the Wight Knight.

"The fuck?" shrieked Solonja as she leaped toward it, sword raised high. His own weapon clanged against hers with effortless power, flinging her bodily to the ground.

The knight glowered over her. "You participate in your own systemic oppression," he spat with disgust. Casually, he tossed the dragonhead over his shoulders and offered Solonja an outstretched hand. "Come, we must rid the land of these cold-blooded tyrants who have infringed on your reproductive rights."

From where she lay, Solonja swung at his bulging calves. The knight lifted his leg with grace to avoid her blow then connected his foot with her chin in the same motion. When the stars cleared, she assumed a sitting position and spat blood. Perhaps this was one foe better defeated by wiles.

"You do realize," she said, "that there are vast biological differences between humans and dragons. Right?" She wiggled a loose tooth with her tongue.

The knight howled. "You raise their young. Everything you do is for their benefit—and to satisfy the Dracriarchal Gaze. You are only reinforcing their control over you. Take back the world where you can be a proud woman."

Solonja let his words hang in the wind. As that gust echoed off the mountain, she heard a wingbeat from afar.

"I was saved by dragons. From men," she said. "The Queen of Flame gave me dignity, power, purpose. I worship at her talons because I have seen the devastation of all in her path. She comes now, for you have just slain her daughter."

The knight turned his shriveled face skyward. His whole body was engulfed in shadow. He raised his sword in the air just as Solonja's own brand tore through his bare torso from behind. She wrenched upward to his throat and back down to split his loins in twain. Then she tore her stolen blade free and dashed from the camp just as a torrent of liquid flame deluged the Wight Knight's body with the heat of a star and the scorn of a grieving mother.

Dread Solonja survived, bearing her stolen sword, and a burden of troubling doubts. Perhaps the river had been cursed after all...

FORBIDDEN FUTURES

DEICIDE
STEVEN L. SHREWSBURY

"To you your father should be as a god."

-WILLIAM SHAKESPEARE

"Remember what we were told," Avan shouted, though his voice shrilled, restricted by the noose about his throat. "Remember the face of your father?"

The crowd about the man on horseback exchanged a few looks. A man with red hair stepped from the throng, the man who'd put Avan's head in the noose minutes before.

Avan didn't wait for him to speak, shouting back, "You know the truth. You know what my father, Balor, had become."

Voices in the crowd shrilled, "Avan slew our god!"

"Avan killed God himself!"

"He struck him down from behind like a coward!"

"With his father's spear! The fabled lance of Goreni from Zorn!"

Avan spat and struggled with the bonds that held his arms behind his back. "That thing dying over there is no god." Steam billowed from his mouth and the horse shifted its hooves in the slushy snow. "Who is it really?"

All eyes aimed at the creature on the ground by the tree, a spear still in its frog-like head, bleeding out a black fluid.

"Look close," Avan yelled. "Does that god of the pole not wear trousers? Does he not dress in the buckled garments of one more familiar?"

The red haired warrior nodded and said with a grim tone, "You seek to deceive us."

Avan retorted, "Corey, you asshead, you can see those are the pants and buckled belt of my father, Balor. Ever wonder why he was the only man who could call forth the spawn for Aphoom-Zah, the thing from the pole of ice?"

"Balor returned with the magick of Zah to conjure the god," Corey affirmed and all in the crowd guffawed. "Only he bore the words for eternal life. He bade us to give the virgins to the god for blood and food; thus, our crops were blessed."

"You're dumber than owlshit," cursed Avan. "I returned from afar to find you fools a slave to this monster, listening to the words of my sire, and giving him whatever he asked."

"You speak blasphemy," Corey declared. "We tribes of the ice and snow revel in our god, the blessed of the Outer Gods."

Avan snarled, "You speak out of your ass. My father was a good man once, as we all were. A trip changed that, huh? Whatever happened to my father up there near the Pole of ice, he returned with the means to get a god to appear, aye? Ever see them together?"

While the crowd muttered, Corey said, "I tire of your words. You will swing and all will be better, save we have no god." He turned to the others. "Mayhap we dine on the god tonight that in the communion of his flesh, we will absorb his life and knowledge?"

Avan started to laugh and shake his head, but then he stopped his actions, glaring at the body of the reptilian deity clad in a man's pants.

No words were needed to get the tribe to stare where he faced. The greenish skinned god shook, then glowed an emerald hue before a clear fluid coursed about the body. The form trembled, then seemed to exhale and grow smaller, drawing inward. Soon, the head of the god faded and melted, taking on a humanoid shape. The rest of the physique also shed the scales and claws of the beast, refining back into the digits and skin of a regular man.

"Balor," the crowd hissed over and over, as their eyes told the tale.

"See?" Avan exhaled and tried to breathe. "There he is, the face of my father. He deceived you all, as the god and beast in the sacrifices given."

Corey walked over, pulled the spear up and out of the ruined head of Balor. "The chief is no god, and dead as part of the deception." He looked up at Avan. "You knew him simply because of his trousers and belt?"

"One never forgets one's father."

Nodding, Corey said, "I see. I shan't forget the face of mine." He looked at the spear, the fabled weapon from the gods of the ice. "And you came back from your journeys and slew our god, slew our chieftain, in fact?"

"Yes," Avan admitted with a sigh.

Corey said, "From your words of honesty, we are cursed in the puddle of truth that runs from his ruined veins, accursed from the creature at the pole he met. The man who beat cyclops and chimera in his lifecycle became what he hated, a monster, a false god."

Avan said gently, "Yes."

"Still," Corey sighed. "You slew god and chief, and thus…" He struck the horse on the ass with the flat of the spear and the animal darted.

Avan swung and the tribe danced. Avan danced with them for a bit.

Too Much Wizard Business
JESSE BULLINGTON
EXILED FROM MIDDLE EARTH

TIME RAN SHORT FOR MELLIFLUVIAN THE PERPETUAL. THE PROCUREMENT OF CERTAIN VITAL COMPONENTS HAD PROVEN MORE TAXING THAT EVER BEFORE, AND RETURNING HOME HE FOUND THE ARCHED BRIDGE TO HIS OWN TOWER BLOCKED BY THE SKELETAL LEGIONS OF HIS OLD RIVAL JORD TODESTONE.

Before, Mellifluvian would have soared over the revenants, not deigning to break a sweat over a few bones, but his dramunculus steed had recently shed its wings, and compensating with sorcery was out of the question. Mellifluvian's peerless powers had already swollen too much to be safely contained in his failing flesh, and if the floodgates opened but a sliver it would all come rushing out, draining him as swiftly as a wineskin at a wizard's moot. No, his only hope was to clear the path to the velvet-draped altar at the top of his tower the old-fashioned way, and once safely ensconced rush through the Rite of Permanent Prolonging before he succumbed to his own potency and began vomiting up spells.

At first blush Jord's undead gambit appeared juvenile, but as Mellifluvian did a headcount of the thralls between the safety of his tower and his current position upon the mountain road, he had to admit simplicity had its allure. The only prize a wizard sought more fervently than immortality was to deprive his peers of the same, and preventing a ritual from going off in the first place was easier than killing an immortal. If these bone boys waylaid Mellifluvian but long enough for his increasingly volatile magicks to crack his overtaxed mortal vessel he was as dead as one of Jord's toys.

"Not so foolish after all," he murmured, though honestly, Jord' most deplorable quality was his cunning. He had been the one who inspired Mellifluvian's method for obtaining immortality, though of course Mellifluvian had improved upon the formula—you could

barely say Jord qualified as immortal at all, the parasitic bacterial intelligence burning through hosts as fast as the Windigo Princess milled through handmaids. Mellifluvian's elegant solution was a newt of a different hue, his sorcerous superiority as plain as the familiar beard spilling down from the increasingly human face of his dramunculus. Little more than an extension of its rider, it looked back at Mellifluvian. Staring into his own eyes, the Perpetual was struck, as always, by what a lovely shade of void they were. He got that from his father.

"Enough dawdling." Mellifluvian drew his cursed hellblade, grimacing to hear his words echo out of the dramunculus' serpentine throat. He'd really put things off to the last possible moment this time.

Sloppy. Mellifluvian and his dramunculus raised their swords, and with a sweep of his majestic cape they stormed their own gates.

Shrieking skeletons barred the bridge, clattering their clavicles in challenge. Wizard and dramunculus swept through the pack like a white-hot needle chasing sentient pus around a petri dish. They were through the scrum and behind the portcullis in no time…but Mellifluvian had less than no time at all, and while his bite wounds were only skin deep the peril he faced extended to his ageless soul.

Up the spiral stair, Mellifluvian! Wheeze into thy plush temple! Unpack the sacred unguents, whose challenging acquisition kept you so late from your tower!

Tripping out of his corpse-torn robes as he lit the lewd candles ringing the mirror-ceilinged shrine, Mellifluvian felt his heat as never before. The dramunculus hopped onto the altar, coyly smearing the lotions upon its steaming vent. The ritual's window had nearly closed, his shrinking draconic simulacrum now physically indistinguishable from Mellifluvian, save for the globular gut hanging down to its wrinkly thighs, and the radiant keyhole between.

"Get on with it," the dramunculus scolded, as if he had forgotten the all-importance of transferring the sum of his consciousness and cosmic power into its new receptacle, along with the traditional biological elixir to fertilize the dramunculus' waiting egg…the sole thorn in Mellifluvian's methods was that his first experience in each new body was the strained laying of his dramunculus successor, but then birth is always painful.

Yet as Mellifluvian grasped for his burning staff it sloughed off between his fingers, crumbling to the carpet like a fondant minaret breaking free from a castle made of cake. Before both sets of his lovely, horror-struck eyes, the corruption spread from pouch to paunch. Too late Mellifluvian realized the slyness of his adversary. Jord hadn't planted reanimated corpses in his path, but the geased victims of some pox that boiled flesh from bones…and first manifested, as all the worst plagues do, in the loins.

"What shall we do?" cried the dramunculus.

Mellifluvian tried to answer, tried to think, tried to control the warring tides of pestilence that ate him from without as his over-fermented sorcery inflated him from within…and failed. The eruption of lifetimes of accumulated power not only blew the hat from his head but the roof from his tower, raining incandescent foulness upon the land.

Not for the first time—but unfortunately, for the last—Mellifluvian the Perpetual finished before he had even properly begun.

2600

2643

2662

2673

2685

2700

LAST DEFENDERS HIDE
BEHIND CASTLE WALLS.

FUTURE FANTASY
2018-2800 A.D.

685 A.D. THE LAST STAND

STAR CHILDREN BREACH THE FINAL BARRIER
ENDING THE GOLDEN AGE OF THE ELVES

FORBIDDEN FUTURES 3
2000
2100
SPRING-
WATER
SANTA
GARRETT COOK
34

MORE METH THAN MAN WAS THIS PURSUER, MORE FROTH WRATH RABIES, MORE DESPERATION THAN REASON AND RELATION TO THE WORLD. THIS MAN HAD GROWN ROOTED TO ALL THAT WAS 82ND, POISONS SEEPING UP AND IN FROM THE ASPHALT, THE PHLEGM AND THE PISS AND THE BLOOD, SPIT AND TRAUMA HAD TAKEN THE PEOPLE PARTS OUT AND REDUCED HIM TO AN AUTOMATON OF STIMULUS AND RESPONSE, THE SORT OF THING TO PUNISH THE EGREGIOUS SIN OF WEARING A SKIRT BUT LOOKING TOO SHARP, TOO STRONG, TOO ANGULAR TO STICK A DICK IN WITHOUT CHANGING OUT A PAPER-THIN AT-LEAST-I-HAVE.

"Faggot!" The junkie screamed at Kylie, and at the moment of lust experienced before seeing she was not quite right, somehow.

Not the first, not the last, but urgent. She needed to lose him. He was going to rape her, he was going to punish her, he was going to break her down and kill her for being who and what she was. The trail was just ahead, like the bridge from sleepy hollow; maybe, just maybe, the evil would fade if she was close enough to home, burn out as if taken by daylight. She was fast, but she was hungry. He had business, urgent business to attend to.

"Stop!" She screamed back, "there are people out here! There are houses!"

"Faggot!" Spat the methman, a word that was now not a word, but a bark of a beast on the hunt that he'd turned into.

Even with the visceral threat, the words crept up her spine. She wanted to scream back, "I'm a fucking girl," but the shouting and the disapproving gazes she had gotten that day on the street, the shoulders too broad, her legs too thick and strong, even if that strength was what kept her out of his reach. He was following it up now with some kind of rant. She could pick out the words "rapist" and "in the asshole." He was laughing too, but it sounded more like braying and coughing.

The grass was growing higher, his shouts joined by the croaking of frogs and the sound of night birds. Five minutes off 82nd, she was back in the woods. Civilization was so much more flimsy than she used to think it was, breaking down both on and off the streets. Closer now, and she hadn't shaken him off all the way. She was leading him right to family. Shame on her. She was taking him into their camp, their woods, where 82nd broke down and they were free. She felt ashamed, now.

Skye would have shouted back. Skye would have gotten up in his face and made him back off like a little bitch. Skye had three inches and fifty pounds on her, but that didn't matter, Skye was powerful inside too, stronger than she could ever be. She might have been bringing him to Skye to fix and that was shameful, that wasn't love, that was fear for her life, that was being too small and too big at the same time, and she'd had enough of that.

"Please!" she shouted back at him, "We're like you, we're just doing what we have to!"

His reply was no longer quite intelligible, the words and noises were running together. He was making monster sounds, now. She was trying to talk to a person, but he only talked monster. She was like him only in her desperation,

and in the places she felt it wasn't safe to be seen. She resigned herself to knowing he was close behind, and he wasn't going anywhere. The camp was in sight, now.

"Please," she tried again, "leave me alone."

A cluster of tents, five of them in a circle. Skye was in one of them. Skye would have kept him away, and maybe outright kicked his ass. But that wasn't important. She had crossed the threshold and now, she was among family and now, she was probably safe. Someone would step out and help, most likely.

They knew and loved her for what she was, even if she was only just becoming it. They too were only just becoming it. She longed for the safety of the cocoon they wove together.

"You can go now," she snapped at him, "you don't want to stick around."

"Faggot!" it growled and she froze up, hunched down into fetal position.

Face between her knees, eyes closed, she felt small and insignificant, as if the family she'd built with all these other queer runaways would come down to nothing, in the face of the rabid junkies of the city that was all too close. She shut down and floated from herself as the next few sounds she heard revealed what was going down. Loud footsteps.

A shriek. Something dragged along the ground. She returned to her body only when she felt the hand on her, bringing her into the tent.

"You did good," Skye told her, "and you were fair. I love you."

"I love you," said Kylie, "I don't…"

Skye kissed her forehead, tenderly and somehow without condescension.

"It won't be your turn for awhile."

Skye slept soundly, but sleep didn't come for Kylie. She felt guilty, she felt cruel, she felt unclean, even if she had been fair. She lay her head on her partner's chest and while the family she'd made all slept, Kylie just waited. She didn't want to read, she didn't want to smoke up or drink, she didn't want to fuck.

She didn't want to think of the dreams she'd have if she managed to get to sleep. She didn't want to step outside the tent, not til daybreak, which took forever to come.

Skye awakened and led Kylie out to the middle of the camp, where everyone had gathered. There was a neat pile like there usually was. Snacks. Two hundred dollars. A bottle of Old Crow. Hormones to go around. The city would give and take, but the woods were willing to trade.

FORBIDDEN FUTURES 3
FEEDING TIME
J. DAVID OSBORNE
36

Jose set aside thirty minutes each day to feed his demons.

He usually did it in the morning. After a cup of coffee he'd fire up his four wheeler and sweep his property, using the .22 to execute the coyotes caught in his traps and the thirty ought six to scare away the kin of the dead pacing the perimeter. Back home, he'd put on his blue-blocking glasses and check to make sure that his aluminum siding had held back the tide of 5G throughout the night. He'd set up two chairs: one for him, and one for the demon. Then he'd light some frankincense and myrrh and whisper a prayer to Jupiter and meditate. After focusing on his breath and imagining himself as a healing wave that spread through his room out the window into the dry dirt and scrub and deer meat that stretched for miles outside his desert cottage, he would dig deep to find whatever troubled him that day.

Usually, it was some form of OCD. A rock that needed kicking or a light switch that wouldn't sit right until it had been turned on and off seventeen times. He would personify that fear and it would appear as a nervous, twitchy man with tentacles for legs or thumbs that twiddled so fast he could barely see them.

The day that he died, however, the demon presented itself as not one solitary being, but as a whole family. Jose pictured a jungle with snakes in wet black dirt and sweating leaves and jaguars vocalizing through the humidity. The leaves rustled back and forth and a family of sasquatch emerged glistening.

The father stood nearly seven feet tall, muscular and covered in sweat. Halfway between ape and man. A powerful hand rested on the mother, shorter and stockier than the male, but just as strong. And between them stood a boy, already as tall as a human man, looking at Jose curiously.

Jose asked them what they wanted. The boy took a seat in the chair opposite. His parents began rummaging through his trailer, knocking pots and pans off the stove, sniffing the contents of his crock pot, rifling through his bedsheets and laying his guns out on the old brown carpet.

The boy didn't respond. Instead, he reached out and touched Jose's hand. The creature's palm was rough yet slick. He grabbed tightly until Jose thought his bones might break.

After his parents were done ransacking his trailer for food, they guided him outside. The air felt charged with electricity. Jose shocked himself on the siding of his home.

The family of Sasquatches led Jose out beyond the perimeter of his property, up a caldera to a spot where he could see the purple mountains stretched out into the distance where they disappeared under grey clouds. For a moment the landscape changed and Jose saw hundreds of the Sasquatches, all of them painted in ochre sigils and praying to a sky god. The family joined the crowd and turned back to Jose and bowed.

He ranked these as the strangest demons he'd ever seen. When he confronted his depression, he'd found it to be a black tentacled beast with thousands of teeth and a guttural voice that told him everything he'd worked for would be for nothing. He'd been terrified of it, but he'd completed the ritual, turning himself into a soft honey made of acceptance that the beast could lick up until it felt satisfied. Since then, he'd woken up every day with a sense of purpose and a sense that he'd made the right choice to move out to the middle of the New Mexican desert, away from his IT job and his wife and his teenage son, now in high school. He knew that he wasn't made for this world and that he could do the least amount of harm away from modernity.

The beasts swayed back and forth, their chants reaching a fever pitch. Jose didn't understand what they represented, or how he was going to feed all of them. All the same, he focused on communicating with them, on finding out what it was they needed.

And as soon as they had appeared, they were gone. The jungle disappeared as well, the wet fronds sucking back into the black bark that ducked under dry dirt. In a moment, all that was left was the desert and the mountains and the sky pregnant with rain.

The coyotes surrounded him. Twelve of them in a circle. The first one moved tentatively, got ahold of his ankle and began to tear. Jose screamed, kicking at the animal with his free foot. The monsters had left all of his guns back at home.

A coyote came up behind him and sank its teeth into Jose's throat. As the rest moved in to consume him, he saw his blood leaking out across the cracked earth and he knew he'd feed them the way he'd fed so many demons before. With nothing left inside of him, he had only his flesh to offer.

2000

2100

DEATHTRAP STEFANIE ELRICK

SO DEATH'S JUST LIKE GIVING BIRTH, BUT BACKWARDS. ALL INWARDS THRUST. REVERSE ACCELERATION. DANGEROUS. CONFUSING, 'COS YOU'RE TRYING TO BREAK BACK IN, SEE? YOU'VE BEEN THERE BEFORE, BUT DIDN'T HAVE THE FEAR THEN: A LIFETIME INSIDE YOUR MEAT CAGE'S MADE YOU SOFT. YOU'VE GOT ONE SHOT TO DIE WELL, SO PEDAL TO THE METAL, BUCKO! QUIT WASTING TIME!! WIN YOUR PLACE OR SCUTTLE BACK INTO YOUR NON-LIFE; ANOTHER GHOST-ROACH SLIPPING THROUGH THE CRACKS.

I never knew this, so count yourself lucky. I'm giving you a head start.

Oh, and if you thought flicking the V's at God in life was clever, think again, 'cos us unbelievers are at a distinct disadvantage. We run the gauntlet; a Hadean race the Godly-gullible get to bypass because they're all on luxury cruise ships, sipping White Ambrosia Russians, mainlining straight to the Almighty.

There isn't any room in their Shangri-La, get it? So believe in something, anything, or end up drag racing down Shit Alley, in the bowels of a R'ylehian spaghetti junction.

'Cos of course, they made it a sport.

It starts with a bang like a faulty exhaust, not some slow celestial exhale. No blissful oblivion, no trippy drift as hot air leaches from your bronchi. No. A bang. An upwards explosion, making your ribs and torso concertina into your neck. Your subtle body starts churning like dirty bath water, rushing towards a penny-wide slit in your forehead. That meager gap glugs you back, sucking you down some pineal sinkhole, before spitting you back out behind the wheel of your shell-shocked soul.

Mine's a banger, an auto-shop mongrel badly welded together. The windscreen's cracked and both wing-mirrors hang off like multiply-fractured arms. It's a stick shift, of course, with all the traction of a coat hanger in a mud pie, and the dial already says I'm low on juice.

Past contenders pile high in stacks of catastrophe around the track.

Not everyone competes in a car.

To my right is a redhead in a chariot, complete with spear and polished shield. To my left: a guy in a gypsy caravan, a black girl on a hover-board and a baffled punk trying to trade a broken pogo-stick. Poor bastard. We make our own crosses, I guess.

A gun shot fires. I slam my foot down. This hunk of junk careens full speed in reverse. I steamroll the punk, who splatters on my hub caps, shrieking as he's banished into anarchist limbo. No time for regrets, 'cos Warrior Queen's a-rolling, followed by Hover-girl with unexpected gusto. The gypsy doesn't make it

more than twenty feet, 'cos a crater with teeth opens up underneath him. I have to move quick, or be the next digested. It crunches his pony, then splinters the wagon. I wrench my gears and speed round its chomping maw.

With a little luck, I might just stand a chance.

Mz. Chariot's way ahead, but lucky for me she's in some trouble, caught in a freak patch of sanguine quick-sludge. Her cart won't budge and her horses are struggling; all that gilded splendor weighing her down. I'm overtaking as she launches a spear over her shoulder, aiming straight and true at my windshield. Braking, the spearhead misses me by inches, before I screech to a stop just short of a vertical drop. Below me, a bubbling swamp pit, where hordes of drowning (or waving?) slop-fiends writhe.

The redhead's resourceful, cutting one of her mares free, then jumping from cart to horse. She gallops away with newfound speed whilst my engine splutters and stalls. This sad sack of rust shows some mercy on the seventeenth try, just as the gore-drenched ghouls learn how to scale the embankment.

Twenty, thirty, forty miles an hour! Boy, I'm really picking up sped!! Then I note a Stargate-sized web just above me, Hover-girl squirming in its center. Her gyrations court a great arachnid beau, and I don't wait to see that sticky end.

Beyond, on the lip of the horizon, a hole's opened up in the sky. The ovum of Eternity, the eclipse of the Great Mother Womb, throbbing like a wet dream for all pilgrims true. I put my foot down, 'cos I'm almost at Xena's heels. She kicks her steed and prepares for the final leap. I ram with a twist, buckling her horse's spindly legs, then rev, charge the jump and howl with glee.

But alas, some malevolent cryptid rises from the mulch below me, and is that Boudicca flying high just ABOVE? It wraps its suckers around my roof and chassis whilst she clears its squamous dimensions on swan-white wIngs. GODDAMIT, if that woman isn't classy! Like some unflinching glory-bound Valkyrie!!

I shake my fists as the monster-fish devours me.

This is the second frikkin time I've died today.

MOWTH
DAN WEBB

MY DAD HAD A TOUGH TIME GROWING UP. He was one of the first interspecies children. His mom, my grandmother, was a student of classical mythology. She had developed a fascination with the myth of the minotaur and fantasized both about having sex with a bull and raising a minotaur offspring. She failed to realize that even though Dad would have human intelligence he would not fit into human society because of his enormous strength. She named him Asterion, after the minotaur of legend, but he chose the name Bruce. Bruce killed one of his pure human friends at age five during a minor fit of rage over the ownership of a doll. Despite extensive counseling and medication, this occurred again when Bruce was seven.

My grandmother retreated to an isolated Pacific island to raise Dad. She was his constant companion, teaching him about the world that feared him through computer screens. He grew huge. Mighty and sad. Grandmother died under mysterious circumstances when Dad was 16. The computer monitoring was down on the island during a particularly rough typhoon. When the storm passed Dad signaled for help. Grandmother's body was spread through the complex. Dad swore that a monster had risen from the sea and attacked them. He fought hard but claimed that a tentacle blow to the head left him unconscious. Although he did have a serious bruise in his horn area—consensus was that a strange act of incest between mother and her monster son had ended my grandmother's life. For the safety of all involved, the island was declared off limits. Pallets of food were air-dropped regularly, and Dad was left to fend as the only one of his kind.

Dad took up art briefly making at first paintings and then later sculptures of the creature that attacked his mother. A giant eel with four tentacle-like arms—the paintings were an artistic sensation for years. Dad would trade them for art supplies. Prominent psychologists analyzed the art as Dad expressions of guilt—leading to a brief neo-Freudianism in 2115.

Dad became convinced that he could trap the monster and thusly clear his name. Taking a page from myth he built an elaborate labyrinth on the island. He hid within hoping that the freak storm that had decimated the island would come again. In 2120 he was rewarded. A massive storm passed over the island and things emerged from the depths. He caught one. A prime specimen.

A blue and black female 14 meters long. Dad was going to kill it and then call a press conference. It did not occur to him the being may be sentient.

Dad had forged an enormous two-handed blade for this procedure. He opened the stone door of the trap that held the long beast. He raised his weapon ready to revenge his mother via decapitation. He paused savoring the relief the deed would cause.

Please no hurt. Please sorry.

The beast had a limited telepathy. It was indeed the creature that had killed my grandmother. It was unaware that surface creatures had sentience and had thought grandma a rather soft and tasty morsel. It understood the urge for revenge since its own kind had complicated blood feuds that lasted for generations but wanted to express both its sorrow and the ignorance of its deeds.

"It" was Illtherya, a minor noble of an ancient space-faring racer. A few members of its kind had been trapped in a crash on earth ten thousand years ago. Illtherya was seven hundred years old. She was a poet, a priestess, and a warrior of her clan. She waited for death, but Dad spared her. She released her back to the ocean. He thought of telling the world but knew that humans would descend to study, to dissect, to experiment.

Illtherya returned on nights of the full moon. Despite their vast physical differences, she and Dad found love. Dad being very genetically unstable was able to impregnate her. Two years later in a live birth in the water I, Mowth, came into being. I grew rapidly spending copious amounts of time in the water as I feed nearly constantly. Dad of course told no one—knowing that I would be a prize specimen for human research. He taught me as his mother had taught him. My mother taught me the ways of her people. The secret names of the stars. The nature of other life in the cosmos.

At first I was much more like my father because he is of this planet. But as I age I become like my mother's people. I can sense their movements between the stars. I have developed the ability for long range telepathy, a genetic trait thought long since lost. Soon I will be able to call across starry space and summon my people.

They will come to the vast seas of this world. They will come, and I can get revenge for what was done to my father. I can put things aright.

Until that day comes I dwell in my father's labyrinth and dream red dreams.

IN EARLY 2325 human population had once again outstripped the Earth's capacity to feed and house them, raising memories of the mass starvations of 2093 and 2222. The restoration of the Earth's seas which had for centuries provided the algae basis for human food suggested an even closer interface with humans and algae might be desirable. The kelpie race standing at the height of one meter and somewhat deficient in IQ (averaging around 85) could be produced by intensive gene therapy in eight-year-old humans. Using projected usefulness as a criterion, "special" children were culled from the human herd and sent to the Green Factories where they were regrown. The process was described as pleasant rebirthing—a re-entry into a green womb where the new embryo would lose her red blood, her memories of land life and become a creature that lived in sensual bliss. Every wave was said to be a caress, the filtering of sunlight down through the seas was described as orgasmic.

The actual process was terrifying, being not unlike a drowning. Extensive surgery came next on an assembly line wherein bones were removed, and a more flexible framework derived from shark cartridge was implanted. A few weeks of computer-directed re-education followed—making the kelpie into a robot-like algae farmer with a simple language (derived from dolphin speak) and a rudimentary religion of service. The kelpie were designed to be sterile.

The first decade of the project went well. The kelpie did recover from the shock of their treatment and their purpose in the ecosystem did give them lives of pleasure. Linguists noticed that their language developed swiftly, and aqua-anthologists noted that the kelpie developed a rather extensive song based culture. This was seen by most land dwellers as a sign of the humanness of the project—millions were saved from starvation and became the aesthetically pleasing little singing nymphs. A few dissenters— notably Dr. George Dorn—suggested that kelpie IQ was not 85 but tending toward 130. He suggested that the kelpie had contacted earlier human aquatic species—this lead to the end of Dorn's career as the "crazy mermaid guy."

IN 2351 the kelpie census came up two disturbing facts. There had been 2.5 million human children that had been transformed into kelpies and located in the tropical and semi-tropical salt water areas. A robotic survey identified 4 million kelpie in these zones. Another unrelated study of ocean current discovered

that kelpie existed as far north as the Arctic ocean. They had gained the power of reproduction and were adapting.

At that time human-kelpie communication occurred regularly to deal with algae farming and maintain oyster beds. When asked about their change, the kelpie laughed at the humans saying that they had always reproduced and been everywhere in the water. Some general alarm ensued stopping the program for two years, but the consensus was the kelpie were helpful and happy—and could not possibly pose a threat. Some studies were made of the offspring who grew only to 0.75 meters in length and had more pronounced ithyic features. Linguists found that they could no longer understand a great deal of kelpie speech which appeared to be tied to ritual and religious activities.

IN 2366 freshwater kelpie appeared— even shorter at .5 meters. The first known attack on a human being was ironically at Loch Ness. Two kelpies broke the surface of the Loch to sing to a human child, Sophie McCheng who was lured into the Loch. Her body was never recovered. Initially seen as an isolated incident over two dozen attacks occurred worldwide over the next six months. The targets were invariably unattended human children. The last of these John Mgumbwae in Kenya was discovered hours after the attack half-transformed into a kelpie. He died in open air, his lungs having ceased to function.

Kelpie population was estimated at ten million.

Algae farming soon ceased and the kelpie began demanding that humans leave the earth so that remaining land masses could be covered with water.

Human aquaculture was transferred to Mars, and an extensive deep-sea war was waged against the kelpie—apparently with great success. Humanity agreed to never pursue forced genetic manipulation as a survival strategy.

After a century of no kelpie sightings, the Pacific Ocean erupted with thousands of space craft of a rather sophisticated design. These departed toward the galactic center. Two pods were shot down and found to be full of vast schools of tiny kelpie (.1 meters). How they had obtained the technology to create the pods in such a brief time—as well as the materials base to do so would haunt humanity for decades. Two watery earth-like planets have been found with kelpie colonies. It is unknown if this is all of them or parts of a watery empire, rich, vast and strange.

KELPIE

DON WEBB

THE GLITCH
RIOS DE LA LUZ
2643

WHEN THE GLITCH BUZZES IN AND OUT OF HER EARS AND VIBRATES IN HER CHEST, SHE WAKES UP INHALING THE EARTH BELOW HER. IN THE CENTER OF A MOSSY FOREST, SHE STARTS PLANTING SMALL SEEDS SHAPED LIKE PYRAMIDS. SHE WAITS FOR THE SEEDLING TO WRIGGLE AND STRETCH OUT. BURSTING EMERALD LEAVES AND MAGENTA BULBOUS BUDS CANOPY OVER THE GROUND AND SLITHER ONTO THE TREES. THE BUDS SHAKE OPEN AND EMIT SMALL GOLDEN SPARKS ECHOING DING! DING! DING! AS THEY POP ONE BY ONE.

This is her earthling trap. This is how she keeps her belly satiated. The glitch happens again and she is back on her home planet, a barren red orb with the purest purple skies and tremendous thunder booming into the core of the planet before exploding into veins in the sky. Thunder used to make her nervous, now it makes her wonder what her next meal will taste like.

The first time she caught a human, she wasn't sure if the creature was edible. A human hand reached through one of her blooming magenta flowers on earth and teleported onto her planet, bursting from underneath the soil. She caught the hand with her spinneret and pulled the body with her fangs after latching onto the creature's wrist.

Covered in red dirt, the creature was pale and immobile. She sucked on the salty fingers and decided it wasn't half-bad. She opened her jaw and fit the entire hand into her mouth. A tingle on her tongue, in her abdomen, and then in her claws. The sensation sent a surge of pleasure into every inch of her body. She moaned as she ate. She bit into one of the forearms. Her head began to spin and she saw stars. The blood was refreshing and she reminisced about a time when her planet was filled with juicy creatures waiting to be sacrificed to her.

When she was done, she felt an explosive impulse to hunt another. She sent one of her children through the parted petals of a magenta flower and it crawled through until it reached the earth.

Her children were obedient and temporary. She lost them every new moon cycle. She wasn't sure how many she had lost at that point and even in her starvation, she refused to eat them.

Her child waited in the forest until a human showed up. It followed the salty, meaty entity and hunted with precision. Her child opened its mouth and with two silver fangs, it penetrated the belly of the prey and dragged it back to its mother. She tore the prey, limb by limb and the human moaned as though it were enjoying itself. It kept screaming as blood gushed and filled the fractured red dirt below. The mother shared with her children and beamed with pride as they tore at the human and shared their meal.

The glitch buzzed, she was teleported onto earth once again, she landed in a yard surrounded by a white picket fence. She planted her pyramid seeds and wandered toward the building. She broke through the walls and ambled into the home. She saw two creatures sleeping, she dragged the smaller one by the foot and waited for her garden to bloom. The human flailed and screamed when it looked up at her.

She used her silk to bind the small creature's eyes, mouth, and then the body. She lifted the limp creature and stuffed it into one of the magenta flowers. The glitch buzzed. She was back on her home planet, nourishing her children, giving them a simple pleasure in case they weren't meant to survive.

EXILED FROM MIDDLE EARTH: *HOW FANTASY FAILED US*
UNCLE KRUST'S DUNGEON BASTARD'S GUIDE TO FANTASTIC BEASTS

CODY GOODFELLOW has written seven solo novels and two more with NY times bestselling author John Skipp. Two of his collections, SILENT WEAPONS FOR QUIET WARS and ALL-MONSTER ACTION, both received the Wonderland Book Award. He wrote, co-produced and scored the short Lovecraftian hygiene film STAY AT HOME DAD, which can be viewed on YouTube. As a bishop of the Esoteric Order of Dagon he presides over several Cthulhu Prayer Breakfasts each year. He is also a co-founder of Perilous Press, an occasional micropublisher of modern cosmic horror.

SPRINGWATER SANTA

GARRETT COOK is an author and editor of horror, Bizarro and cosmic horror fiction. His most recent novels are A GOD HUNGRY WALLS and CRISIS BOY.

DEICIDE

Award winning author STEVEN L. SHREWSBURY writes hardcore sword & sorcery and horror novels. Twenty of his novels have been published, including BORN OF SWORDS, WITHIN, OVERKILL, PHILISTINE, HELL BILLY, THRALL, BLOOD & STEEL, STRONGER THAN DEATH, HAWG, TORMENTOR and GODFORSAKEN. His horror/western series includes BAD MAGICK, LAST MAN SCREAMING and MOJO HAND. He has collaborated with Brian Keene on the two works KING OF THE BASTARDS and THRONE OF THE BASTARDS and Peter Welmerink on the Viking saga BEDLAM UNLEASHED. A big fan of books, history, guns, the occult, religion and sports, he tries to seek out brightness in the world, wherever it may hide.

THE GLITCH

RIOS de la LUZ is a queer xicana/chapina sci-fi loving writer. She is the author of the short story collection, THE PULSE BETWEEN DIMENSIONS AND THE DESERT (Ladybox Books, 2015) and the novella ITZA (Broken River Books, 2017). Her work has appeared in VOL 1 BROOKLYN, THE FEM LIT MAGAZINE, ENTROPY, LUNA MAGAZINE, CORPOREAL CLAMOR, AND ST. SUCIA.

FEEDING TIME

J. DAVID OSBORNE lives in El Paso, TX. He is the host of The JDO Show, available on iTunes, *thejdoshow.podbean.com, brokenriverbooks.com.*

WIGHT KNIGHT

NATHAN CARSON is a writer, musician, and Moth StorySlam Champion from Portland, Oregon. His nonfiction can be found in the pages of WILLAMETTE WEEK, THE OREGONIAN, RUE MORGUE, NIGHTMARE MAGAZINE, DECIBEL, and countless other outlets. His fiction has been published in a constant stream of weird horror anthologies and magazines. STARR CREEK is his first standalone book. His recent graphic novel adaptation of Algernon Blackwood's THE WILLOWS is on comic stands now. Oh yeah, he is also a founding member of Portland's first doom metal band, WITCH MOUNTAIN, now celebrating its 20th anniversary. More info at *www.nathancarson.rocks*

TEARS OF ELOHIM

JOHN R. FULTZ lives in the North Bay Area of California. SON OF TALL EAGLE is his fifth novel, following 2015's THE TESTAMENT OF TALL EAGLE. His Books of the Shaper trilogy includes SEVEN PRINCES (2012), SEVEN KINGS, and SEVEN SORCERERS (2013) from Orbit/Hachette. His short fiction has appeared in YEAR'S BEST WEIRD FICTION, WEIRD TALES, BLACK GATE, WEIRDBOOK, SKELOS, THAT IS NOT DEAD, SHATTERED SHIELDS, LIGHTSPEED, WAY OF THE WIZARD, CTHULHU'S REIGN, et al. *johnrfultz.com*

DEATHTRAP

STEFANIE ELRICK is a writer, artist and performer from Manchester, UK. As a performance artist she's blood-lined love poetry onto her body during 'Written in Skin' www.writteninskin.com and been strapped to a 12ft spinning timepiece for 'KAIROS' www.kairosophy.com. She made her literary debut in Martian Migraines Press CTHULHUSATTVA: TALES OF THE BLACK GNOSIS and featured in Comet Press's 2017 THE YEAR'S BEST HARDCORE HORROR as well as Apex Magazine's August 2018 Zodiac themed issue. Things are just starting to get interesting. *stefanieelrick.com*

MOWTH
KELPIE

DON WEBB was born on Highway 66 on Walpurgisnacht 1960. A nominee for the International Horror Critics Award, the Shirley Jackson Award and the Rhysling Award he is an expert in not winning things. He has had 22 books published and a day job as a Special Education teacher. He once dated a woman that Madonna also dated. He has worked a pyrotechnician.

DRAGONCEL

CHAD STROUP received his MFA in Fiction from San Diego State University. SECRETS OF THE WEIRD, Stroup's debut novel, is available from Grey Matter Press, his second novel, SEXY LEPER, is forthcoming from Bizarro Pulp Press, and his debut comic series, HAG, is forthcoming from American Gothic Press. His short stories have been featured in anthologies such as CHIRAL MAD 4, LOST FILMS, SPLATTERLANDS, AND CALIFORNIA SCREAMIN', and his dark poetry has appeared in all volumes of the HWA Poetry Showcase. Visit his blog Subvertbia at http://subvertbia.blogspot.com/, follow him on Instagram (@chadxstroup), and drop by his Facebook page at *facebook. com/ChadStroupWriter*

TOO MUCH WIZARD BUSINESS

JESSE BULLINGTON is the author of three weird historical novels: THE SAD TALE OF THE BROTHERS GROSSBART, THE ENTERPRISE OF DEATH, and THE FOLLY OF THE WORLD. Under the pen name Alex Marshall he recently completed the Crimson Empire trilogy; the first book, A CROWN FOR COLD SILVER, was shortlisted for the James Tiptree, Jr. Award.

ARTWORK

Graphic Novelist and Illustrator MIKE DUBISCH, known behind his back as Doob, has been creating and publishing comics and art since the 1980's. Hailing from a family of scientists and mathematicians, Dubisch has carved out a unique place for himself in the world of fantasy art, creating a timeless oeuvre using all but lost traditional art techniques. Born in California, USA, the artist has traveled the world and lived in five countries. Dubisch has been an instructor at the Academy of Art University since 2012, and is married to children's book illustrator and sculptor Carolyn Watson Dubisch, with whom he has three daughters.

ODDNESS

Author, Publisher, Producer originates from unknown lands, and dabbles in modular synths and playing video games.